Little Red Riding Hood

TORMONT

Graphic design and illustrations: Zapp
Story adaptation: Robyn Bryant

© 1995 Tormont Publications Inc.
   338 Saint Antoine St. East
   Montreal, Canada H2Y 1A3
   Tel. (514) 954-1441
   Fax (514) 954-5086

ISBN 2-89429-844-7

Printed in China

Once upon a time, there was a girl named Amanda who lived in a village near a forest. Whenever she went out, Amanda wore a red riding cloak, so everyone in the village called her Little Red Riding Hood.

One morning, a messenger brought a letter. "Oh dear," Amanda's mother said when she read it. "Your grandmother is not feeling well."

"Homemade soup might make her feel better," Amanda suggested.

"That's a good idea," her mother said. So they packed a nice basket for Amanda to take to her grandmother.

When the basket was ready, Amanda put on her red cloak and kissed her mother goodbye.

"Remember, go straight to Granny's house," her mother said. "Don't wander off the path! The woods are dangerous."

"Don't worry, mother," Amanda said. "I won't."

But when Amanda noticed some flowers in the woods, she forgot her promise. She picked a few here, and a few there, and soon she strayed quite far from the path. She never noticed the wolf.

After a time, she ran into the village woodcutter. "What are you doing all alone in the woods, Red Riding Hood?" he asked.

"I'm picking some flowers for Granny. She's sick," Amanda said.

"Well, you had better get back on the path," the woodcutter said. "A wolf has been seen in the area."

The woodcutter led Amanda back to the path. But a few moments later she saw some butterflies, and followed them into the woods. Suddenly, the wolf appeared beside her. "What are you doing out here, Red Riding Hood?" he asked, for the wolf had heard the woodcutter call her that.

"I'm on my way to see my Granny, who is not feeling well," Amanda explained.

"Well, you had better let me take you back to the path," the wolf said. "There is a wolf in the neighbourhood, you know".

"What does a wolf look like?" asked Amanda.

"Oh, they have very long purple ears,"
said the wolf. "And where does your dear
Granny live?" he asked.

Amanda told him precisely, for she
was a polite girl, even if she was not
very obedient. Then she continued on
the path to Granny's house. The wolf,
in the meantime, took a shortcut.

$\mathbb{T}$ he wolf, a little out of breath from running, arrived at Granny's and knocked on the door.

"Who is it?" Granny called from her bed.

"It's Red Riding Hood," the wolf replied in a high sweet voice.

"Oh, how lovely! Do come in, my dear," said Granny.

So the wolf let himself in. Poor Granny did not have time to say another word, before the wolf gobbled her up.

The wolf let out a satisfied burp, and then poked through Granny's wardrobe to find a nightgown that he liked. He added a frilly sleeping cap, and dabbed some of Granny's perfume behind his pointy ears.

When he was all dressed, he posed in front of the mirror, and practiced Granny's voice. "Oh, how lovely! Do come in!" he croaked, until he was satisfied.

A few minutes later, Red Riding Hood
knocked on the door. The wolf jumped
into bed and pulled the covers over his
nose. "Who is it?" he called in a cackly
voice.

"It's me, Red Riding Hood," Amanda
replied.

"Oh, how lovely! Do come in, my dear,"
squeaked the wolf.

Amanda put her basket on the kitchen
table, and gave her granny a kiss on the
cheek. "Poor Granny," Amanda said.
"You don't look like yourself at all! I'm
going to make you a nice hot lunch."

"That sounds lovely," said the wolf.

"Your voice sounds loud and scratchy," Amanda said as she sliced some bread.

"Oh, well. The better to greet you with, my dear," said the wolf.

"This soup might help," Amanda said, bringing her a big bowl. "We made your favorite, chicken."

"Thank you, dear," said the wolf.

"Are your ears bothering you too, Granny?" Amanda asked, noticing the lumps in Granny's cap.

"Perhaps they are a bit swollen. But the better to hear you with, my dear," said the wolf. But as he spoke, the nightgown slipped from over his nose.

"Oh my!" said Amanda. "Your teeth are so big!"

"The better to eat you with, my dear!" roared the wolf.

In a flash, Little Red Riding Hood had joined her granny in the wolf's belly.

The wolf burped again, and lay down for a little nap. But he snored so loudly that his snores caught the attention of a passing hunter.

"Something seems to be the matter with Red Riding Hood's grandmother," the hunter decided.

The hunter knocked on the door, but the wolf was sleeping so soundly that he did not waken.

The hunter then pushed open the windows. As soon as he saw the wolf asleep in the bed, he fired his musket and killed the wolf in one shot.

The hunter wanted to make sure that the wolf was dead, so he listened for a heartbeat. Instead, he heard faint voices crying for help. He cut the wolf open. Out stepped Red Riding Hood and her Granny, safe and sound.

"Oh Granny, I was so scared!" Amanda said. "I promise I will never wander off again!"

"You have learned an important lesson, my dear," her Granny said.

A little later, the hunter escorted Red Riding Hood back to her house.

"Oh, there you are, Amanda," her mother said. "How is your Granny feeling?"

"Much better now," said Little Red Riding Hood.